BATTY RIDDLES

by Katy Hall and Lisa Eisenberg

pictures by Nicole Rubel

Dial Books for Young Readers · New York

Published by Dial Books for Young Readers
A Division of Penguin Books USA Inc.
375 Hudson Street
New York, New York 10014

Printed in Hong Kong
by South China Printing Company (1988) Limited
The Dial Easy-to-Read logo is a registered trademark of
Dial Books for Young Readers,
a division of Penguin Books USA Inc.,
® TM 1,162,718.

Library of Congress Cataloging in Publication Data
Hall, Katy. Batty riddles /
by Katy Hall and Lisa Eisenberg ; pictures by Nicole Rubel.
p. cm.
Summary: A collection of riddles about bats, including
"Why did the little bat walk around in his pajamas?
He didn't have a bat robe!"
ISBN 0-8037-1217-0. ISBN 0-8037-1218-9 (lib. bdg.)
1. Riddles—Juvenile. 2. Bats—Juvenile humor.
[1. Bats—Wit and humor. 2. Riddles.]
I. Eisenberg, Lisa. II. Rubel, Nicole, ill. III. Title.
PN6371.5.H345 1993 818'.5402—dc20 91-20777 CIP AC

The paintings, which consist of black ink and colored markers,
are color-separated and reproduced in full color.

Reading Level 1.8

EASY
READER
E
H
3/94

To all the kids who drive us batty—
Leigh, Kate, Annie, and Tommy

K.H. and L.E.

To my Batty husband

N.R.

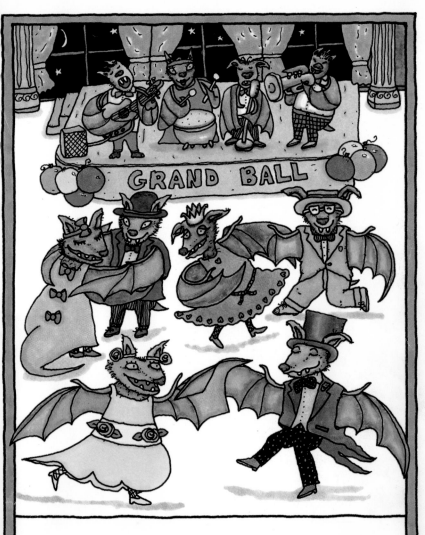

What do you get if you cross
a vampire and a big dance?

A bat ball!

Why did the vampire bat's girlfriend break up with him?

She thought
he was a pain in the neck!

What did the little bat say
when she was asked to dinner?

"No fangs, I just ate!"

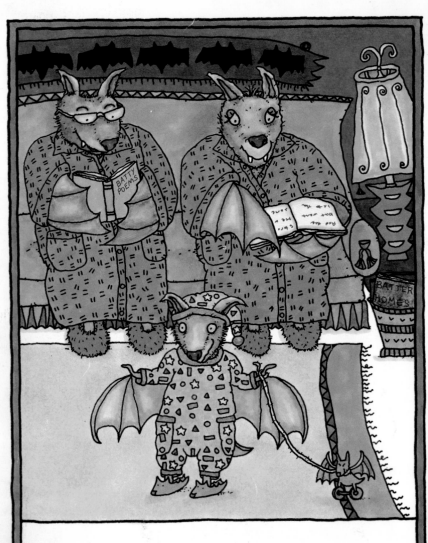

Why did the little bat
walk around in his pajamas?

He didn't have a bat robe!

Why did the little bat
use mouthwash?

She had bat breath!

When do bats squeak?

When they need to be oiled!

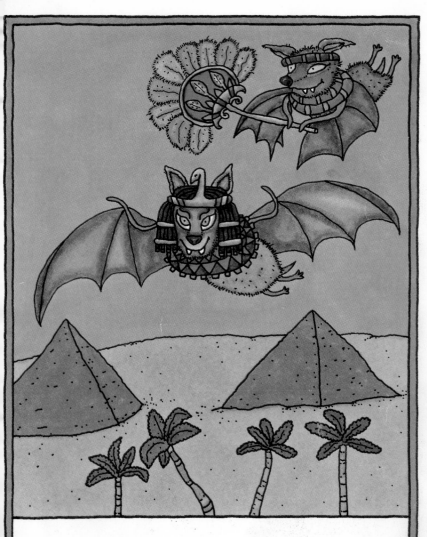

What famous flying mammal lived in ancient Egypt?

Cleobatra!

Why did Junior Bat
want to get a job?

He was tired
of just hanging around.

Why did the baseball player strike out?

He was using the wrong bat!

What did the little bat
do in school when she didn't
know the answer?

She just winged it!

Why did Mom Bat
hate the letter "r"?

Because it turned
her baby into a brat!

What fruit do
vampires like best?

Neck-tarines.

Where are you most likely
to find bats in your house?

In the bat-room.

What do you get if
you cross a ball with a bat?

A home run!

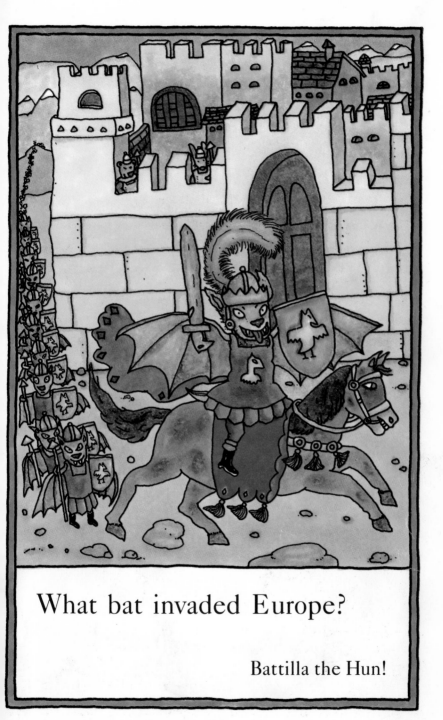

What bat invaded Europe?

Battilla the Hun!

Where do bats go to gamble?

Batlantic City!

Which bat hangs the highest?

The acro-bat!

23

What happened when the
little bat swallowed
the doorbell?

It turned into a dingbat!

What is a vampire's favorite animal?

The giraffe.

What kind of car does a vampire drive?

A bloodmobile!

Why did the vampire
cross the road?

It was attached to
the chicken's neck!

What do you get when
you cross a frog and
a flying mammal?

A creature that says,
"Ribbat, ribbat!"

What game do baby vampires like to play?

Batty cake, batty cake!

Which bat knows its ABCs?

The alpha-bat!

What do you get if you cross
a bat and a hatchet?

A battle-ax!

What bat makes
your camera work?

The bat-tery!

What holiday do
bats love best?

St. Batrick's Day!

Why couldn't the little vampire play baseball?

He was only a bat boy!

What do you get
if you cross a vampire
with a snowflake?

Frostbite!

What flying mammal might you find in a Paris church?

The Hunchbat of Notre Dame.

What position did
the little vampire play
on the football team?

Quarterbat.

What do you have to know
to teach a bat tricks?

More than the bat!

What do you call a dream
about a vampire chasing you?

A bitemare!

What kind of dogs do vampires like best?

Bloodhounds!

What game do little batties
like to play with little birdies?

Batminton!

Why didn't the little bat
laugh at the joke about
the cave?

It was too deep for him!

Why should you never let
a vampire into your car?

It'll drive you batty!

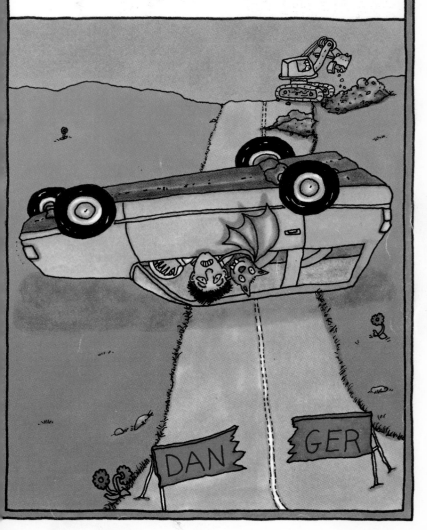

What do you get if you cross
a bat with a woodpecker?

Bat-a-tat-tat!

What bat hero wears a cape
and can leap tall buildings
in a single bound?

Swooperman!

What do you call vampires
that cheer you on
at football games?

Bat-on twirlers!

What bat sewed the American flag?

Batsy Ross!

What do you say when you come to the end of *Batty Riddles?*

"Bat's all, Folks!"